Five Children and It

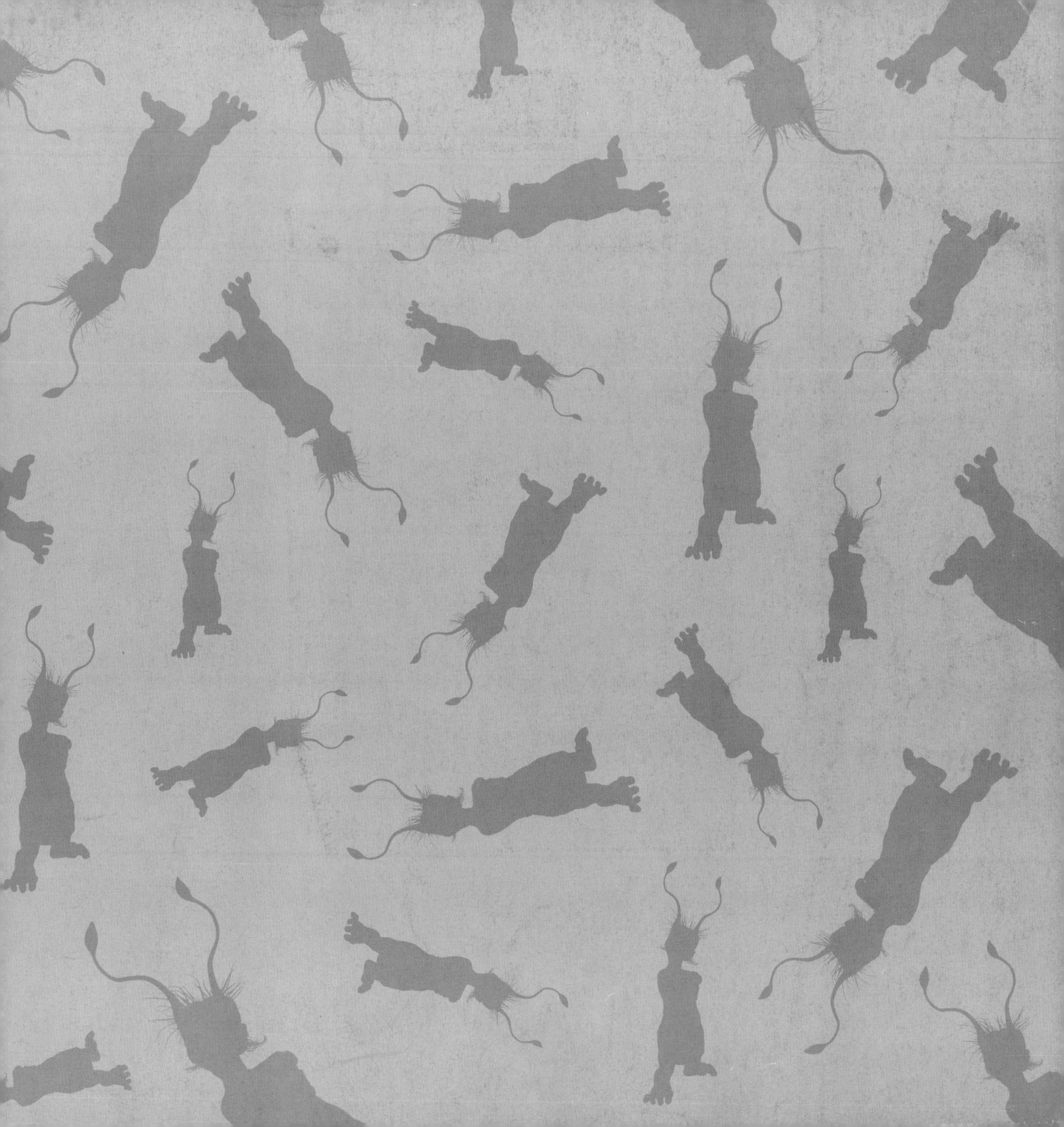

Capitol Films and the UK Film Council present in association with the Isle of Man Film Commission and in association with Endgame Entertainment a Jim Henson Company Production a Capitol Films/Davis Films Production FIVE CHILDREN & IT Freddie Highmore Zoë Wanamaker Eddie Izzard as the Voice of It and Kenneth Branagh as Uncle Albert Casting By Michelle Guish Gaby Kester Costume Designer Phoebe De Gaye Composer Jane Antonia Cornish Production Designer Roger Hall Edited by Michael Ellis A.C.E. Director of Photography Michael Brewster Co-Producer Kathy Sykes Executive Producers Jane Barclay Kristine Belson Steve Christian Victor Hadida Sharon Harel Robert Jones Hannah Leader Jim Stern Screenplay by David Solomons Produced by Nick Hirschkorn Lisa Henson Samuel Hadida Directed by John Stephenson

First published in Great Britain in 2004 by HarperCollins Children's Books.
HarperCollins Children's Books is a division of HarperCollins Publishers Ltd.

1 3 5 7 9 10 8 6 4 2

Unit Photography by Liam Daniel.
'It' Character Effects and Animation by the Jim Henson's Creature Shop.
Additional Visual Effects by Lola
Adaptation by HarperCollins Publishers

Based on the Motion Picture Screenplay by David Solomons

Based on the original novel by E.Nesbit

0-00-719689-X

The HarperCollins website address is: www.harpercollinschildrensbooks.co.uk

Printed and bound in Italy.

Five Children and It

HarperCollins *Children's Books*

Gather round children, grab a piece of sand and let me tell you a story.

It's all about wishes and magic, and five pesky children I met one summer.

And, before you ask, I'm a Psammead – or sand-fairy. What?! I don't look like a fairy? How dare you!

Well, I may not have wings, but I can grant wishes. That's right, I can make your wishes come true. Just be careful what you wish for!

How old am I? Well, how rude! Not that it's any of your business but I'm 8,311 years old. Yes, that's right and I do look VERY good for my age, thank you!

You may call me 'IT' – that's what the children called me.

Right, where was I? Oh yes, it was a lovely peaceful day and I was tucked up inside my cosy shell minding my own business. When suddenly…

Some very LOUD shouting woke me up. Most annoying!
I poked my antennae out of my shell and guess what I saw? Five children!
Two boys, two girls and an itsy-bitsy baby one. Well of course I told them to
shove off – I even tried distracting them and running away, but it was no use!
I think I gave them quite a shock! *Hah!* Serves them right for waking me.

Their father was away at war and they were living in a nearby house with their uncle. It seemed I was stuck with them. Just my luck!

Can you guess what their first wish was?

The children wished for help with their chores. What a funny wish!
I gave them an army of lookalikes to polish the house from top to bottom.

But, things didn't turn out quite
as they expected – oh, dear!

Instead of cleaning and scrubbing there was smashing and flooding.

Look, there's a cupboard
full of Janes SCREECHING
on the violin.
What a noise! What a mess!
What *were* they going to do?

Luckily, when the sun goes down my wishes all disappear – *poof!*
Didn't I tell you that? Well, now you know.

The next day those pesky children came back to my beach.
This time they wished for gold – buckets of it.
But what did they do with all that gold?

They went shopping of course! Cyril wanted a bright red motor car. But the test drive was a bit of a bumpy ride!

Toot! Toot!

Crash! Whoops!

I wondered if I had put them off wishing forever?

Cyril said, "No more wishes!" How boring – for me!
You know there's nothing like granting a wish for sand-fairy fun.

Anyway, instead, they played with their cousin, Horace.
Now, I wouldn't wish him on my worst enemy!
Horrible Horace locked Cyril, Anthea and Jane right at the top of the house – in the attic in fact! They were trapped!

Luckily, Robert had escaped and came to ask me for help. Typical!
Of course he wished for wings, so the children could
fly out of the attic window to freedom. Brilliant!
And fluffy white wings were exactly what they got. Oh, I'm *so* good at this!

Where do you think they went?

Up, up and away they flew. Robert thought they could get all the way to France to see their father, silly boy. Uh-oh, they almost crashed into some airships! Those children were always getting in trouble! *How would they get home before the sun went down and their wings vanished?*

It was up to me to help them – again!
A nice big gust of wind blew them to shore just as their wings disappeared.

I didn't have to help but, well, I was getting used to having those children around.
Home safe and sound. But what was their mother doing there?
Something was wrong…

The children's father had gone missing!
Robert raced down to see me.
He needed a new wish – to find his father!

Now as every child should know, rules are rules. My book of wishes clearly says only one wish per day. I told Robert he'd simply have to wait until tomorrow.

So he went to sleep right there, on my shell!
Most uncomfortable I tell you – I just don't do snuggling!

But when Robert awoke,
my shell was empty!

I had been kidnapped, or should I say sand-fairy-knapped!
After Robert dozed off, horrible Horace grabbed me. He tied me up in his scary laboratory. I wasn't really scared but just look at all those yucky experiments!

Ugh!

Robert and the others came to rescue me. Just in time, too!
To distract Horace from turning ME into an experiment, Robert told him I could grant him a wish. The ghastly boy wished for a real live dinosaur! Imagine that, a T-Rex let loose on cousin Horace!

Oh, dear, it could have been very messy indeed... ROAR!

Unfortunately, the children didn't want my dinosaur to gobble up young Horace.
Pity! Jane tried to calm the drooling beast by playing her violin.

What a terrible idea! So, I made my T-Rex disappear.
Waste of a good wish if you ask me!

Phew, that was a close call. After such an ordeal I felt quite faint!

Those kind children carried me back to the beach.
I suppose they're not so bad – sometimes.

What a relief it was to get back to my shell. There's no place like a mobile home!
The one called Cyril wished to see his father again.

Well, even for a sand-fairy of my vast
experience that was one BIG wish.
I had to concentrate really, really hard.
But of course, I did it.

When their father appeared
the children were amazed.
They must have missed him,
such emotional little creatures!

Disturbed again!

Won't those children leave me alone? But this time, they didn't want a wish.

They came to wish me a happy birthday and to say goodbye.
Jane gave me a card and a present. Ah, isn't she sweet?

We had a yummy picnic
and they even brought
me a birthday cake.

Hiccup,

I think I ate
too much!

After our birthday feast we relaxed on the beach.
Ah, that's the life!
Robert says he'll never forget me and he'll always remember his amazing summer.
A summer of magical wishes for five children and… IT.
And I'll always remember this story. Won't you?

It was time to say goodbye, time for the children to go back home. They were leaving that very day. And for your information, I wasn't crying I just had sand in my eye! I'm looking forward to another few hundred years of perfect peace and quiet. Unless of course *you* come across me on a beach some day...

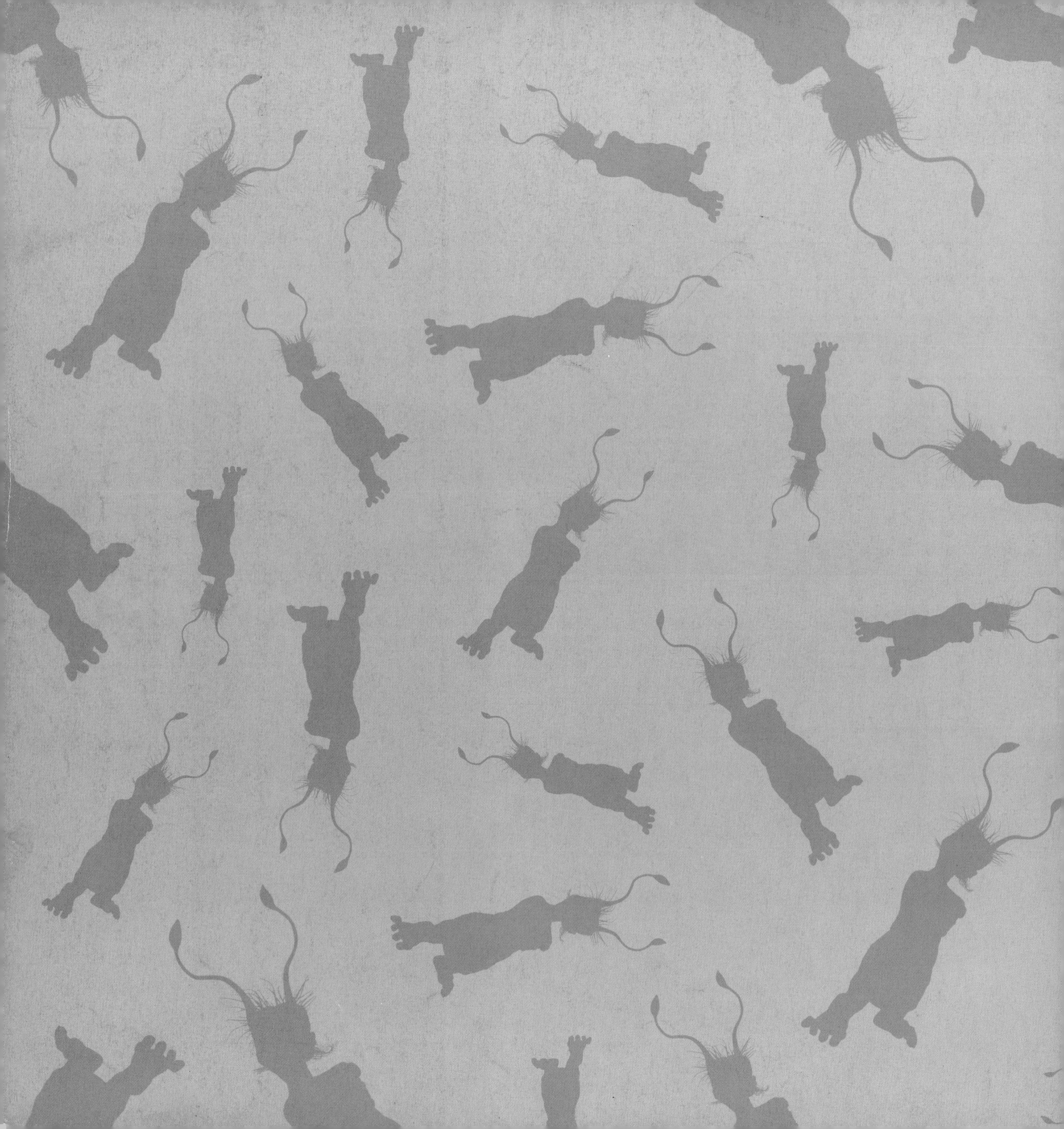

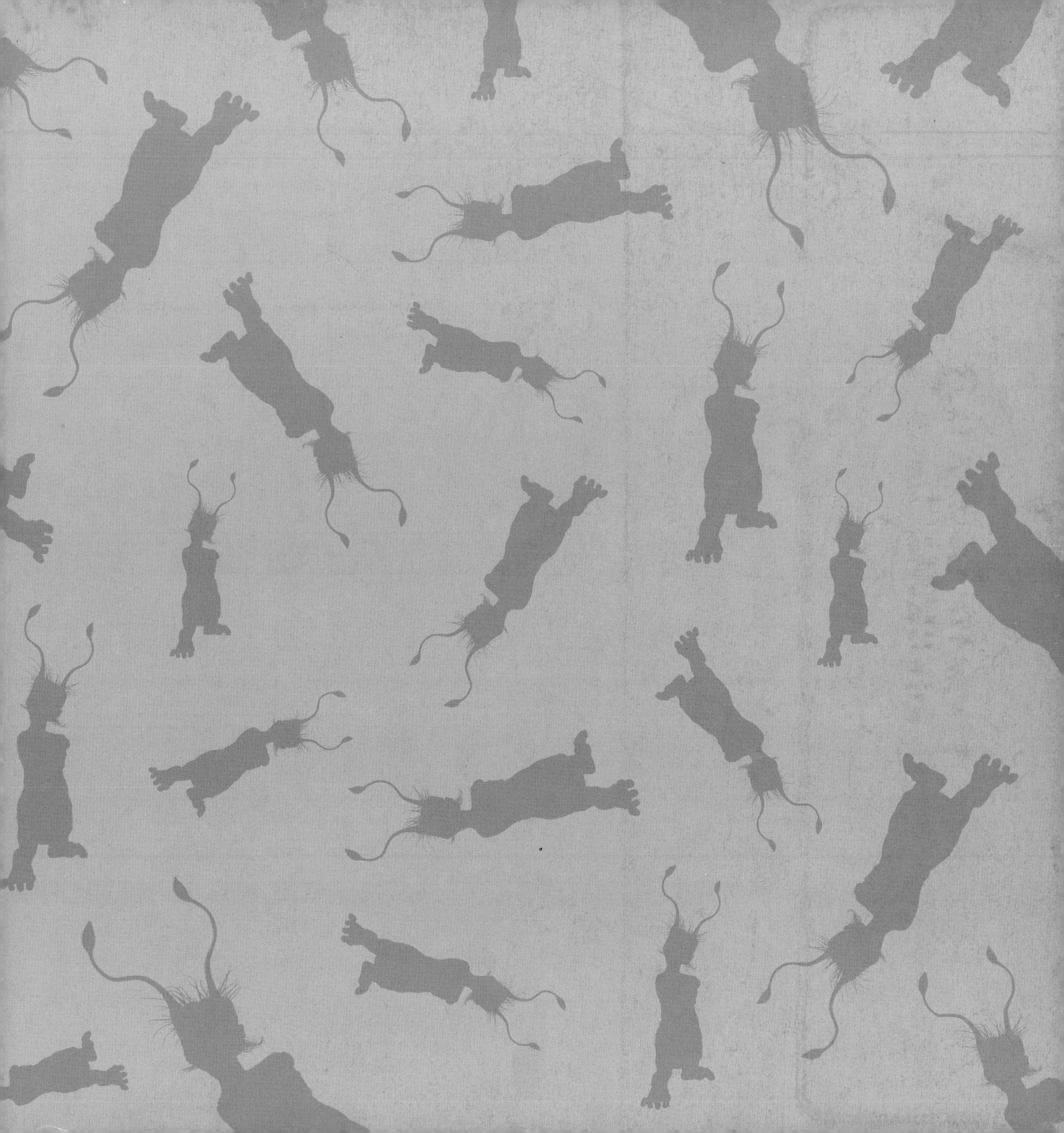